GOLDEN-FRONTED LEAFBIRD:
Although this bird is common in Borneo, it is difficult to spot because of its extreme shyness and tendency to keep to the tops of trees.

BLUE-FOOTED BOOBY: Found only on the Pacific coast of the Americas, these birds have an entertaining courtship ritual in which— much like little soldiers—they march proudly about, displaying their bright blue feet.

PHEASANT: Found in almost every part of the world, this bird spends most of its time walking or running on its strong legs. When startled, it rockets into the air, then glides into hiding.

GREAT HORNBILL: Found in parts of Africa and Asia, this large, ponderous-looking bird has a prominent ridge, or horn, on its large bill. It hops about in a clownish manner while catching its food in mid-air.

GROUSE: This heavy-bodied, chicken-like bird roams through grass and forests of Europe, Asia, and North America looking for seeds and insects to eat. A favorite with hunters, it makes a whirring sound and is capable of great speed and agility.

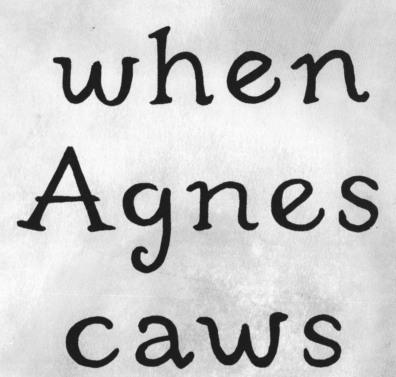

when
Agnes
caws

written by
CANDACE FLEMING

illustrated by
GISELLE POTTER

ALADDIN PAPERBACKS
NEW YORK LONDON TORONTO SYDNEY SINGAPORE

For Scott and Michael, whose outrageously silly
birdcalls were pure inspiration!
—C. F.

For Kieran
—G. P.

First Aladdin Paperbacks edition June 2002
Text copyright © 1999 by Candace Fleming
Illustrations copyright © 1999 by Giselle Potter
ALADDIN PAPERBACKS
An imprint of Simon & Schuster
Children's Publishing Division
1230 Avenue of the Americas
New York, NY 10020
Also available in an Atheneum Books for Young Readers hardcover edition.
Designed by Angela Carlino
The text of this book was set in Lomba
Printed in Hong Kong

10 9 8 7 6 5 4 3 2 1
The Library of Congress has cataloged the hardcover edition as follows:
Fleming, Candace.
When Agnes caws / by Candace Fleming ; illustrated by Giselle Potter.—1st ed.
p.   cm.
"An Anne Schwartz book."
Summary: When eight-year-old Agnes Peregrine, an accomplished birdcaller,
travels with her mother to the Himalayas in search of the elusive pink-headed
duck, she encounters a dastardly foe.
ISBN 0-689-81471-2
[1. Birdsong—Fiction. 2. Birds—Fiction. 3. Humorous stories.]
I. Potter, Giselle, ill. II. Title.
PZ7.F59936Wh 1999 [E]—dc21 97-32921
ISBN 0-689-85118-9 (Aladdin pbk.)

Agnes Peregrine, daughter of the well-known ornithologist, Professor Octavia Peregrine, was a real birdbrain.

At the age of three, Agnes could do the courtship dance of the blue-footed booby.

At the age of five, she could imitate the flight of the yellow-bellied sapsucker.

But it wasn't until Agnes was eight that her greatest skill was revealed. Two days into a bird-watching trip to Borneo, a shriek pierced the jungle air.

"*Cawaak! Caweek! Eek! Eek! Eek!*"

Agnes's mother, Professor Peregrine, whipped out her binoculars. "Did you hear that?" she whispered. "It was the call of the golden-fronted leafbird."

"You mean this?" asked Agnes. "Cawaak! Caweek! Eek! Eek! Eek!"

Out of thin air, a flock of leafbirds flitted to the ground.

"Why, Agnes," declared her mother. "You have a true talent for birdcalling."

"I do!" whooped Agnes. "I really do!"

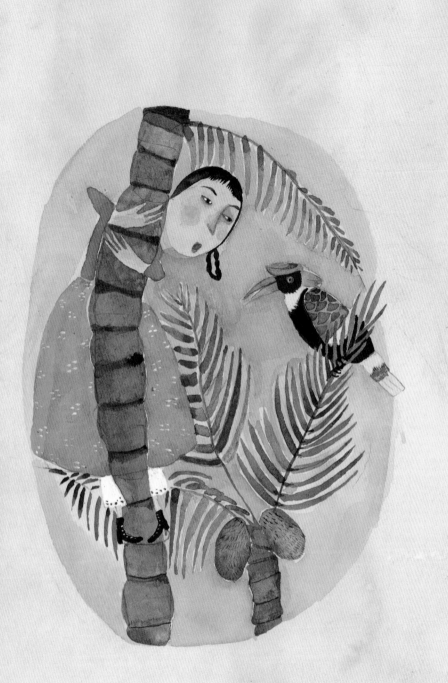

Agnes practiced her skill wherever she went.

On the African savanna she called the great hornbill. "Pee-up! Pee-up! Pee-pee-oh!"

In the rain forests of New Guinea she called the sulfur-crested cockatoo. "Chac-ca-cha-ca! Wick! Wick! Wick!"

And deep in the swampy Everglades she called the sharp-beaked snake bird. "Chup-lup! Chup-lup! Chup-lup!"

In New York City's Central Park she called the ruby-throated hummingbird. "Hmmmmmmmm!"

Agnes's talent made bird-watching easy. It also made news. Reporters, photographers, nature lovers, all went atwitter over the little girl. But the greatest honor came from the World Bird Society.

Its members voted to send the Peregrines
in search of the rarest, most elusive bird of
all—the pink-headed duck!

"Spotting that duck will be a challenge," Professor Peregrine explained. "It hasn't been seen in decades."

"Bet I can call it," said Agnes. "And I bet it will come."

"There's only one problem," admitted her mother. "No one knows what the pink-headed duck sounds like."

"Then I better get quacking," replied Agnes. And she warbled a round of duck calls.

Meanwhile, on the other side of the Atlantic, Colonel Edwin Pittsnap, avid bird collector, sat in his country manor house. All around him were the spoils of his many hunts. Grouse were mounted above the mantel. Pheasants under glass served as end tables. Every nook and cranny was crammed with dead birds.

And Pittsnap craved still more.

Now the colonel opened his newspaper and read about the Peregrines. "A pink-headed duck!" he hissed. "I've so longed to get my hands on one of those. But how? HOW?"

A crooked idea came to him.

"It's deliciously crafty," he cackled. "It's superbly cunning! It's sure to work!" And rubbing his hands over his dastardly plan, he hurried to pack.

The Peregrines also packed. And then they set off on their trek.

By ship.

By train.

By yak.

Until, at last, they reached the far-off slopes of the Himalayan Mountains, home of the rare pink-headed duck.

As soon as they'd pitched camp, Agnes started calling. Little did she know that cleverly hidden on a nearby slope, Colonel Pittsnap watched and waited. . . .

Day after disappointing day, Agnes cawed. Dozens of birds answered, but, alas, not one pink-headed duck.

"This is for the birds," Agnes hollered, fed up, and she kicked a sharp rock. "Ouch-ow! Ouch-ow! Oh drat!" she cried, rubbing her stubbed foot.

"Ouch-ow! Ouch-ow! Clack! Clack!"

The Peregrines looked up. Overhead flew the rare, the elusive—

pink-headed duck!

The little duck flapped to the ground.

"Wow," whispered mother and daughter.

"Now!" whispered Colonel Pittsnap. He reached for his net.

SWOOSH!

"*Ouch-ow,*" cried the duck.

"At last!" crowed Colonel Pittsnap. He darted away with his catch.

The Peregrines were stunned. "Where'd he come from?" Agnes asked.

"No idea," said her mother.

"Hey!" Agnes yelled. "That's my duck!" And she charged after him.

"Agnes!" cried her mother. She charged after her daughter.

It wasn't long before Agnes found herself on a distant slope, closing in on Colonel Pittsnap. Boldly, she stepped into view. "Hand over that duck!" she demanded.

Colonel Pittsnap jumped. He smiled a fake smile. "My, what a surprise," he said in an oily voice. "I came to capture the pink-headed duck, and by chance caught the golden-throated birdcaller, too."

The colonel threw back his head and laughed wickedly. Then, staring hard at Agnes, he demanded, "Call some birds for my collection."

"I won't!" cried Agnes. "You can't make me."

Colonel Pittsnap's nostrils flared. "I have ways of making you squawk," he hissed. And he took a step toward the small girl.

By the look on his face, Agnes knew he meant business. There was only one thing to do.

"Caw! Squawk! Cheep! Chirp! Chacalaca-wooo! Kip-whip! Hoot! Quack! Cock-a-doodle-doo! Twitter-tee! Chup-chup-chup! Wick-wick-wick! Caweek! Gobble-gobble! Ack-ack! Pee-pee-oh! Pee-wee!" she cried.

In a wing's beat, and from all corners of the world, the birds replied—hundreds and hundreds of them. They rose from their roosts. They soared through the sky. And with a cacophony of angry cries, they surrounded the colonel.

"You little fool," screamed Pittsnap. "You called too many!" He swiped at the feathered air, but the birds refused to leave. Grouse buzzed him. Pheasants bombarded him. Around and around, the birds swirled, nipping, poking, pecking, scolding. Around and around jumped Colonel Pittsnap, weaving, swatting, crouching, dodging. And watching it all was Agnes.

Suddenly, into the fray came Professor Peregrine. "Agnes!" she cried. "What happened?"

"He asked me to call the birds," answered Agnes. "So I did."

At that moment, the birdpecked colonel let out a tremendous "Aaaagh!" and made a mad dash down the mountain. The birds swarmed after him.

Professor Peregrine turned to Agnes. "Well done," she praised.

"Thanks, Ma," said Agnes, "but the birds really did it."

Gently they untangled the pink-headed duck from the net.

"*Clack!*" said the duck, ruffling its feathers.

"Clack," said Agnes.

Then, paddling on webbed feet to reach flying speed, the pink-headed duck took to the air and winged its way over the horizon.

"Wow,"
said Agnes.

RUBY-THROATED HUMMINGBIRD:
This tiny bird's wings beat so fast that they
sound like the hum of a bee. Otherwise
soundless, hummingbirds exist around North
America, though the ruby-throated variety can
be found only in the East.

SULFUR-CRESTED COCKATOO: Also
known as the "cage bird," this bird of Australia
and New Guinea is loud and boisterous, and can
be taught to talk.

SNAKE BIRD: Common to the Florida
Everglades, this bird dives beneath the open
waters of the marsh, where it uses its long, sharp
beak to spear fish.

YELLOW-BELLIED SAPSUCKER: This North American bird drills holes in the bark of trees with its beak, then uses its long, brushlike tongue to feed on the sap.

PINK-HEADED DUCK: This duck once inhabited areas of India and Nepal, but because of its unusual, eye-catching colors it was overhunted and quickly became rare. The last official sighting was in 1936, but in the 1960s a group of bird-watchers claimed to have spotted one in Tibet. Today, bird experts think the pink-headed duck is extinct. Still, they keep their binoculars peeled, just in case.